A PANGOLIN TALE: ADVENTURE OF THE ARMORED ANTEATER

978-0-9964891-2-6

www.oakenday.com

Illustrator: Louise Fletcher
Bio: Louise's passion for pangolin conservation initially developed while working with The Carnivore and Pangolin Conservation Program in Vietnam for eighteen months radio tracking rehabilitated Sunda Pangolins. She has seen how inspirational sharing this passion can be through work with other organizations including 1stopbrunei Wildlife Club and The Indonesian Species Conservation Fund on pangolin related projects, and has found this love of nature and wildlife as a wellspring of inspiration for her lifelong passion in drawing and watercolor painting. Louise holds a Master of Science in Conservation and Biodiversity from Exeter University and a bachelor's from Bristol University, both in the United Kingdom.

Author: Jason Derry
Bio: As a child, Jason found joy, awe, and safe harbor in two places above all else: stories and nature. He owes this foundation to his mother, who taught him to see wonder in fireflies, and who would recite made-up tales of scampering mice and flying tennis shoes during those slow summer evenings. Now, Jason is a Communication Studies doctoral candidate at the University of Denver focused on Environmental Communication, and holds a master's degree in Environmental Education and a bachelor's degree in Creative Writing.

For questions about orders, our mission, queries, the sociological research behind what we do, to learn more about the plight of pangolins, or to discuss ideas on how you can make science and ecology playful and fun contact us at info@oakenday.com.

For the pangolins.

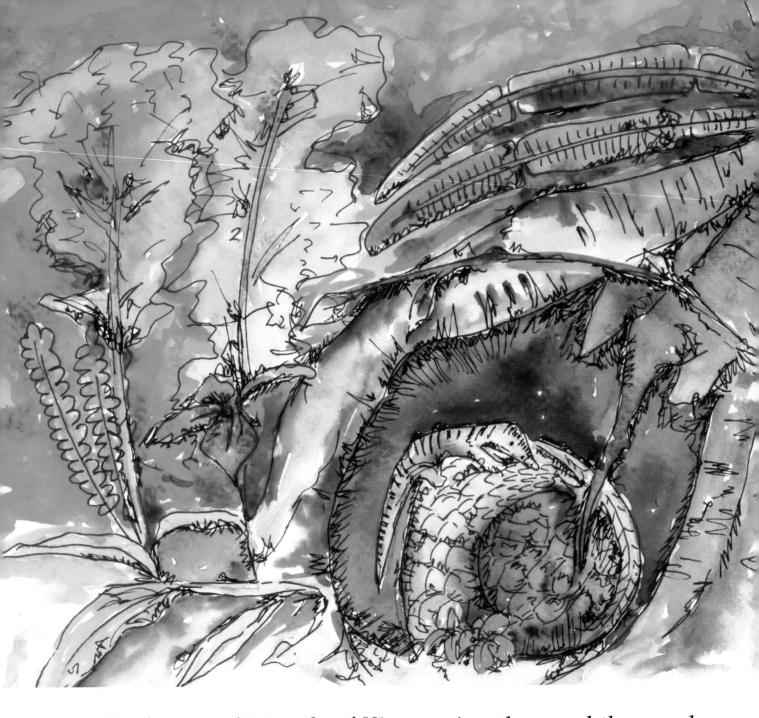

In the moonlit jungle of Vietnam is a thousand thousand trees. In one of the hollows of one of the trees was a pangolin named Nallie, cuddling her newborn pup.

With her belly grumbling for dinner,
Nallie emerged from the hollow in search of food.

Shambling across the leaves and bark, she made
her way along a branch and reached out with
her wiggling nose to smell into the dark.

Suddenly surprised by the grubby scent below, she quickened down the rain-wet trunk and happily across a small stream.

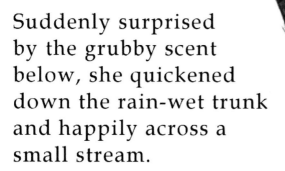

On the other side, she pressed her claws into the mud, like fingers into a cake.

There, what she was searching for – ants.

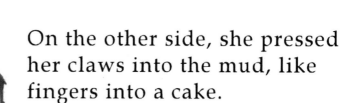

Filling her belly
on the insect buffet,
Nallie turned back
toward her tree.

But suddenly, out of nowhere
she noticed a face - large,
striped, orange and black -
staring directly at her,
motionless.

5

The tiger pounced.

Frightened, Nallie quickly
did what pangolins do best,
and curled tightly into an
armored ball – her scales
a dozen dozen tiny shields.

The tiger tried to bite her,
but her shell was too strong.
It tried to claw her and
uncurl her, but her shell
was still too strong.

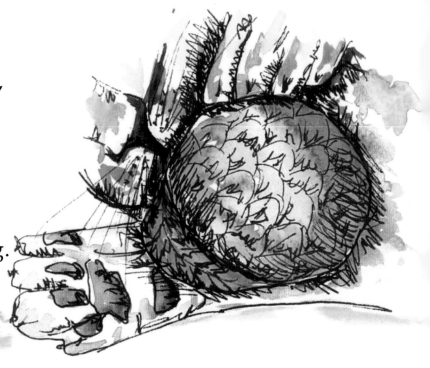

After rolling her downstream, the
tiger, full of frustration, tossed
Nallie into the moon-glimmered
water and meandered back into
the shadowed trees to hunt.

Nallie splashed into the stream
like a coconut, and swam to the
muddy bank.

7

Lost from the encounter,
Nallie stuck her nose into the air.

She smelled the earthiness of the mud,
the fishiness of the water,
the woodiness of the decaying leaves,

but could not smell her pup.

9

Determined, she climbed a nearby tree
and reached out into the air with her nose.
Higher up in the wind, the smell was faint
but distinct, her pangopup, to the north!

10

With dawn quickly approaching,
Nallie hastened down the tree,
her thick tail waving in the air
for balance,

when suddenly a laughing gibbon
swung onto a nearby branch.

11

Nallie looked up at the gibbon as if to say
hello, and the gibbon stretched out and
touched her nose!

Nallie sneezed on his finger – ahchoo!

The gibbon made a gibbony yelp and turned
and swung away with his lanky arms.

12

Still hungry, Nallie brambled down
the tree to the river's muddy edge
and looked north along the river.
The leaves whispered and danced
in the canopy. The final stars faded
from the sky as it brightened a hazy
blue, and the sun birthed from the
horizon's edge just a sliver:
it's bed time for pangolins.

Nearby, bunches of orange ants
billowed across the leaves like
living waterfalls and rivers.

Nallie huffed knowing her pup
was still waiting for dinner, but
excited for the treat, ran to the
crawling clusters, licking the ants
up in large tasty tonguefulls.

14

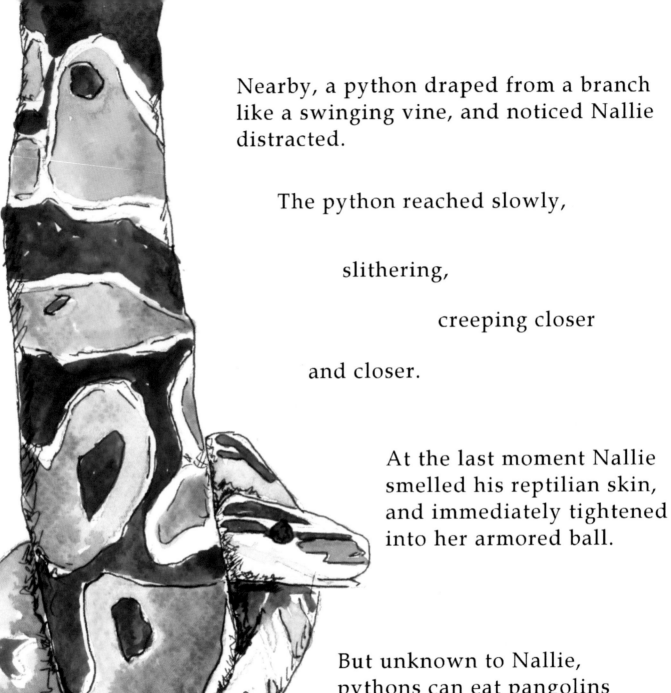

Nearby, a python draped from a branch like a swinging vine, and noticed Nallie distracted.

The python reached slowly,

slithering,

creeping closer

and closer.

At the last moment Nallie smelled his reptilian skin, and immediately tightened into her armored ball.

But unknown to Nallie, pythons can eat pangolins whole, armored shell and all!

Frightened, she remained curled in her aegis,
feeling the warmth of her belly on her nose,

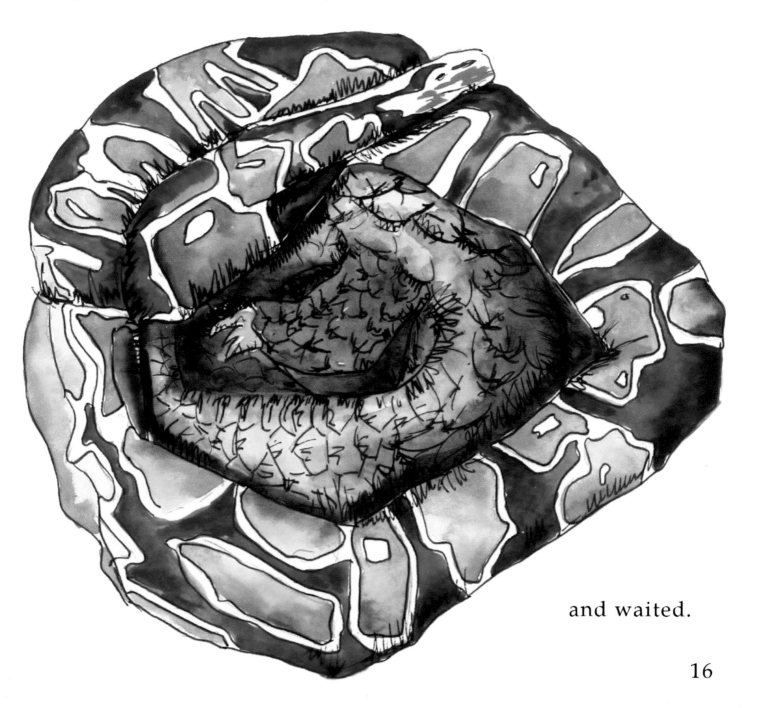

and waited.

Just as the python started to
wrap around her, his own
tiny scales against hers,
Nallie's new gibbon friend
swung down and yelped,
pounding at the ground.

Quickly joining them, a
troupe of gibbons swung
down, drumming the soil
and yelping, their tails
wavering in the air.

Bothered by the drumming,
the python slithered back into the jungle.

Her gibbon friend ran over and laughed, patting her
on the back. Nallie uncurled and the gibbon touched
her nose once more before jumping back into the sunlit
trees with his family.

18

Tired, full, and ready for bed, Nallie sprinted
a silly pangolin sprint along the mudbank
toward home.

Finally arriving, she climbed
quickly along the bark to her
hollow. Her pup squeaked.
She squeeked in return.

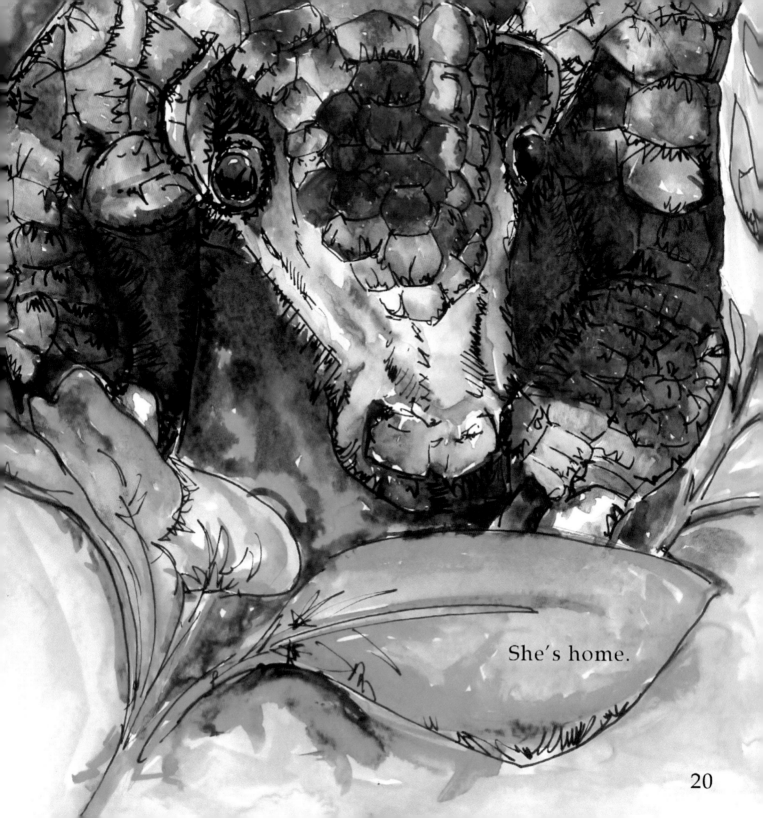

She's home.

The sun gleaned in bright shimmers along the water and the emerald leaves rustled in the wind. Another day has started for the valley as Nallie drifted asleep.

21

Let's
learn about
Pangolins!

Let's
learn about
Pangolins!

As the only mammals with scales, pangolins are quite unique! Found in many places throughout Asia and Africa, there are eight known species with many different shapes and sizes. Some have shorter tails, some longer. Some walk on all fours, some with their back two legs. Seven are nocturnal, meaning they are awake at night and sleep during the day, while one (the long-tailed pangolin in Africa) prefers the daylight. While nicknamed "scaly anteaters," they are actually closer cousins to wolves and lions and dogs and bears than anteaters.

LATE NIGHT SNACK

Unlike many mammals, pangolins don't chew their food! They don't even have teeth. Instead they use their long sticky tongues to collect insects and swallow them whole. Some pangolin tongues can be up to 40 cm (or 15 inches) long! While most nocturnal animals have very large eyes in order to see better in the dark, pangolins have tiny eyes and very poor eyesight. Instead of sight, they rely on hearing and a very strong sense of smell to find termite mounds and make their way around their habitats. To help get at the termites and buried insects, they use their long noses and their very large front claws to dig into the soil. The front claws of the larger African species are so bulky that they mostly walk on their hind legs, balancing with their tail.

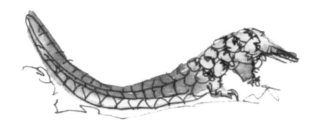

STOP, DROP, and ROLL

Imagine if you had a permanent suit of armor. Unique among mammals, pangolins are covered in hard thick scales made of keratin (the same material a rhino's horn or your fingernails are made out of). The scales are so strong not even big cats like lions, tigers, and leopards can bite through them. Because of this defensive shield, when frightened, most pangolins will curl up into a tight protective ball. In addition to the suit of armor, pangolin scales are very sharp. Like having a tail covered in a dozen knives, occasionally they will swing and slash their tails at predators. If the armor and slicing doesn't scare off potential predators, pangolins can release a putrid smelling oil to gross out anyone nearby.
.

A FAMILY TAIL

Pangolins live very solitary lives, spending most of their time alone. The exceptions to this hermit lifestyle are mating season and when mothers raise their babies. When a pangopup is born, the mother will carry it on her tail for three months, and then watch over it until it reaches adulthood at two years old! Hang on tight pangopup!

YOU CAN HELP

Unfortunately, all eight species of pangolins are threatened with extinction, and two are critically endangered. Even so, they are hunted for their scales and meat, face increasing habitat loss, and are the most trafficked animal in the world. But there are many ways to help! They are quite elusive and still fairly unknown, so learning about them and telling others about how neat they are is a great first step, you can also choose not to eat them or wear products made from their scales, and by getting this book you've already helped us donate toward their conservation!

Learn even more at www.PangolinSG.org and www.PangolinBook.com!

Made in the USA
Columbia, SC
16 November 2019